DATE DUE			

The Saving of
Valiant Blue Heron

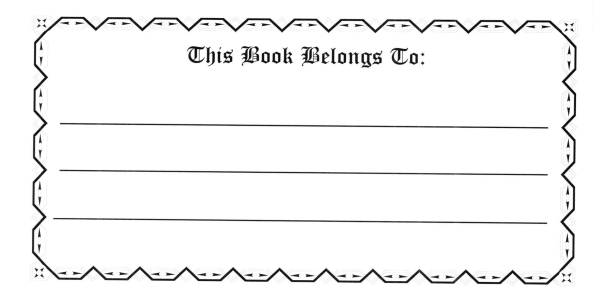

This Book Belongs To:

The Saving of Valiant Blue Heron

by John Harms II

Illustrated by Robin Lee Makowski

Edited by Robert Franklin Spencer

Frederick Press ~ Palm Beach Gardens, Florida

Library of Congress Catalog Card Number 97-90821

ISBN 0-9653871-7-8

Printed in the United States of America

Dedicated to my wife and children,

for the mutual love and interest they share with me in the earth's ecosystem.

Company Philosophy

Frederick Press strives to inspire children to realize the importance of caring for their local environment with a positive active roll. By showcasing interesting animals that are common to areas, children learn to relate to the needs of their own surroundings. They become more environmentally conscious and willing to care for the life that surrounds them. Frederick Press hopes children will become more aware of their natural environment by enjoying the adventures of a boy named Buster and the animals he encounters.

When people take proper care of their local ecology and are responsible when visiting other areas, the earth's environment will improve and be a much better place for all living things.

Frederick Press donates a portion of its revenue to benefit the rehabilitation of injured and orphaned animals, supporting zoological parks, and saving the Florida Manatee.

TABLE OF CONTENTS

*Glossary words are *italicized* throughout the story for easy reference.

CHAPTER 1

~ Another Adventure ~

Buster greeted the dawn. This day would bring another great adventure. The first rays of sun glistened on the lagoon. Without waking anyone, he quietly slipped down to the dock. A long-time had passed since he had seen Arma Armadillo and her twin sister, Erma.

When he reached the dock he stopped to take in the beauty of the day. The sun was just easing over the horizon like a brilliant yellow ball. The sky was a deep blue with small puffy white clouds. The water was so mirror like that, as he dangled upside down from the dock, the reflection of the houses looked as if they were right side up.

"What a wonderful day," he thought as he gazed at the lagoon. He put his old *duffel bag* filled with his lunch, life preserver, and other supplies into his boat while his eyes searched the lagoon's surface. A large round ripple suddenly appeared at the far side. This always excited Buster, for the ripples often meant that a manatee had broken the surface of the water as it came up for air.

Sure enough, it was a manatee!

"I wonder what that manatee's going to do today?" he thought as he started the boat's motor.

He piloted the boat slowly so he wouldn't disturb the manatee. The manatee kept moving steadily toward the *spill-way* to eat its favorite water plant, fresh water hyacinths.

He continued through the lagoon to the woods where Arma lived. The bridge was finally completed, and the temporary dam was removed. The stream was flowing naturally again, the way it did before the construction that caused Arma's burrow to flood.

Buster followed the stream in his boat as far as he could. *Cypress knees* and trees lined both sides, blocking his path. Getting out of his boat, he walked along a path made by deer and other large animals. Hunters called it a game path.

Arma was *nocturnal*, so Buster was hoping she was still awake. "Come on out Arma!" Buster called in his best armadillo sounds.

To Buster's surprise he heard a rumbling in the bushes by the burrow.

"Who is making that racket? Get away from my burrow! I need my sleep," complained Arma. "I'll scare him away before he scares me." Just like some humans, armadillos can be very cranky when they're tired.

"Get out of here! You're bothering me!" she snorted as she bluffed a *charge* from the bushes. "Out! Out!" she squealed as Buster instinctively backed away from the opening.

When she noticed it was Buster; she stopped. "Oh! It's the boy that saved me. Well I'm going to go to sleep no matter who's here, and that's that," she huffed.

"Hi Arma, I'm glad to see you're doing OK. Boy, are you crabby," Buster said laughing as her tail vanished down the opening of her burrow.

CHAPTER 2

~ *Buster Meets Valiant* ~

Continuing down the game path, he came to a large shallow freshwater lake. There seemed to be hundreds of great blue herons and great white egrets wading along the shore. He sat down by some dahoon holly trees to admire the birds as they fished for food.

One of the great egrets moved fairly close to Buster as it cautiously crept up on a fish. Suddenly it stood motionless, stretching its beak out and up at an angle. Then as fast as lightning "SPLASH!"

His head went down into the water, and within a split second, out popped its head with a fish. Flip, flop, flip, flop, tossing the fish until it was head first; he swallowed it. "Yum, Yum!"

Buster figured, "I can fish like that." He took off his shoes and waded into the water. Leaning forward, he put his arms up at an angle toward the morning sun and waited quietly. After what seemed like forever, a mullet swam between his legs and stopped below his head. "NOW!" Buster yelled. "SPLASH!"

As his hands plunged, he felt the fish slip right through his fingers. His feet began to slide on the muddy bottom. The fish jumped and swam away as if it was laughing. Buster tried to keep his balance, but he couldn't. "KERSPLASH!"

All the birds in the lake stopped what they were doing and glared at Buster sitting in the water.

"It's a human!" the birds squawked as they flew away. All except for one. Buster could see that there was something wrong with it. As he watched the great blue heron, he noticed an arrow sticking out of its right wing.

"That bird is in trouble and will get attacked by bob-cats if I don't help him," Buster reasoned.

He waded to shore while keeping an eye on the injured heron to see where it would go. It wasn't long until the birds calmed down and started coming back to the lake. The injured heron continued fishing with the rest. Then an idea came to Buster, and off he raced to his boat.

Reaching his boat, he grabbed his old *duffel bag*, dumped it out, and ran back to the lake. He remembered a program on falcons at the conservation camp. When a falcon had a hood over its head, it became calmer and was easier to handle. With the *duffel bag* over the heron's head, Buster could take him to his friend Jake, the wildlife officer.

Buster began to circle around the flock of birds to get behind the great blue heron.

"Now what's he doing?" a great egret cooed to his mate.

"Let's stay away from him," answered his mate as they moved away.

So even though Buster crept up with the greatest of care, the birds would move farther down the lake's shore staying just out of reach. He followed them halfway around the lake and still couldn't get close enough to help the heron.

"This isn't helping much," he realized. "Maybe I should run after them." So he ran at the flock of birds as fast as he could.

"He's after us! Fly! Fly away again!" screeched the birds as they flew off leaving the injured heron alone with Buster.

"Help! Help! I can't fly!" the heron cawed while running in circles, side stepping away from Buster. "What can I do? What can I do?"

Buster took aim on the run and heaved the bag in the air. "SPLASH!" — Into the water it went! The heron slipped out of its reach and *charged* at Buster. Buster dove out of the way and grabbed the bag before it could sink.

"Well, I guess that's not the way to get a heron in a bag," he admitted out loud.

Next he tried to talk to it softly. "Easy heron, I just want to help you. Easy now, let me put this bag on you. Don't be afraid," Buster said soothingly while slowly walking closer to the bird.

By now the heron was so tired it stood still for a second to conserve its energy, but even with a hurt wing he wasn't going to let Buster catch him without a struggle. This time Buster cautiously slipped behind him. Then slowly he raised his bag.

"You're not taking me that easily!" the heron crowed poking at Buster with his beak as he ran into the water.

By being careful Buster knew he had made progress with the bird. He waited a moment and then cautiously waded towards the heron for the second time. Again he got close to the heron, but the heron moved. After about two hours of playing "catch the heron tag", both of them were worn out.

Buster could hardly lift the *duffel bag* by then, and the heron was so tired he just sat on the ground. When Buster finally got the strength to put the bag over the heron's head, it didn't even bother to peck at him. He pulled the strings on the bag carefully until only its legs and injured wing could be seen sticking out.

"At last!" Buster exclaimed. "You're the toughest animal I have ever tried to help. What can I call you? I know; I'll call you Valiant. Even though you were tired, you courageously kept trying to remain free. Yep, Valiant Blue Heron is your name."

Buster and Valiant sat on the bank for a few minutes resting from all the action. Buster watched as the wonders of the lake unfolded.

The other birds had returned to the mirrored surface of the lake. In the background the cypress trees were mint green from the new spring growth. In the forest, ferns covered the ground like a fluffy carpet. Some trees were polka dotted with white spots caused by the pelicans roosting on them. An osprey was circling above searching for mullet to feed its young.

CHAPTER 3

~ Help For Valiant ~

"Well Valiant, we better get going and get you some help," Buster said while trying to lift the heron. But instead, Valiant stood up and tried to run off again, with the bag over his head! Buster leaped up, grabbed the side of the bag, and Valiant turned towards him.

That gave Buster an idea. He reached into the deep pocket of his camp shorts and pulled out some twine. By tying the twine to each side of the bag, he was able to direct the bird to the boat.

What a strange, funny sight. A bag with bony, skinny legs walking down the shore followed by Buster. When they finally got to the boat, Buster put Valiant in the bow of the boat, pushed off, and headed for home.

When he got to the dock he jumped out and ran to the house. Calling out, "Dad! Dad! There's a great blue heron in the boat with an arrow in its wing. It needs help right away!" Buster's father liked animals too. After all, he was the one who taught Buster to appreciate living things.

After hearing the heron was injured, his dad ran to the boat and gently carried it to the back of their station-wagon.

"Buster, you stay here and watch him. I'll call Jake!" his dad said with great concern.

When his dad came out, they drove the bird to the animal sanctuary hospital where Jake, the wildlife officer, said he'd meet them. There a veterinarian who specialized in birds would be able to help Valiant. On the way, Buster told his dad about catching the bird and why he named him Valiant. As soon as they arrived at the hospital, Jake and the veterinarian took Valiant in and removed the arrow.

"It looks like with a little *T. L.C.* this one will fly again," the vet said coming out of the operating room. "Valiant needs about six weeks here and he'll be as good as new. Hey! If you'd like, I'll give you a call when he's well enough to fly and you can come see him off."

"Wow! Can we Dad? That'd be cool!" Buster cried out with joy.

"Sure we can," his dad said with a chuckle and a pat on Buster's back, "you were pretty brave to help him. We'll see all of you in about six weeks."

After thanking Jake and the vet, Buster said good-bye to Valiant and then he and his dad headed for home.

The moment he got home, Buster counted and marked on the calendar when the six weeks would be up. As the days went by, he called the doctor often to see how Valiant was doing.

Finally the 42nd day arrived! Buster woke up extra early with such excitement he didn't even want to take time for breakfast. Waking his dad he exclaimed, "Dad! Dad! Hurry! We need to set Valiant free. C'mon, I can't wait."

"Now just wait a minute Buster! We need to at least call Jake and the vet to make sure Valiant is ready to fly," his father said grinning while picking up the phone.

After his dad got off the phone, he and Buster jumped into the station wagon and drove to the hospital. Jake met them at the front door.

"We'll take my pick-up truck since Valiant's cage is already set in the back," Jake said guiding Buster and his dad out the back door of the hospital.

Jake's dusty old pick-up sat on the shell rock parking lot looking as if it would fall apart at the next bump in the road. Buster rubbed his hand over the fender to reveal the faded white paint under the mud and dirt.

"Buster, if it's OK with your dad, you can sit in the back with Valiant," Jake said while jumping into the driver's seat.

"Sure, go ahead," his dad said hopping into the passenger's side.

"Great!" Buster said leaping into the rear of the truck.

Off they sped on a logging road toward the lake. Jake stopped the truck on the top of a hill so they could view Valiant's beautiful home.

As Jake and Buster's dad got out of the truck Jake asked, "Buster, would you like to open the cage door for Valiant?"

Buster was so excited that before Jake could finish his sentence; he sprang up, reached for the latch, and threw the door open!

"Fly Valiant! You can fly again …. Fly away!" he excitedly called out.

At first Valiant hesitated, but it wasn't long before he jumped into the air and was off. He circled high above Buster twice as if to say thanks. Then he flew back to the shallow lake where Buster had first found him. Buster even imagined he heard Valiant whoop as he flew, "I can fly again! I'm free! They set me free."

Buster smiled as they all drove back to the hospital. He had helped to save another animal and to him nothing felt better. Feeling contented, he hugged his dad and thought, "Another wonderful day. Another wonderful adventure!"

The End

Glossary

Duffel Bag: A large canvas bag used to carry things.

Spill-way: A barrier built across a canal or stream that regulates the flow of water to help prevent flooding.

Cypress knees: A growth that is peculiar to the cypress trees. A part of the root system that resembles knees sticking out of the water. Scientists still don't know why they grow that way.

Nocturnal: Animals that come out usually at night to feed. Some nocturnal animals are armadillos, owls, and bats.

Charge: To rush at in a threatening manner.

T. L. C. : An abbreviation for Tender Loving Care. This is what all plants, animals, and humans need to heal when they're hurt, including you!

More About Great Blue Herons

"Great Blue Herons" are the largest, growing up to 54 inches in length, and most widely distributed member of the heron family. Some great blue herons migrate from Canada in North America to Columbia in South America, while others remain in one habitat year-round like many that live in south Florida.

The heron is a very patient fisher. Wading to an area that looks good for fish, it stands perfectly still with its neck stretched out at about a 45° angle. When it locates a fish its body seems to fill with tension. Slowly its head comes back into a cocked position as it takes one step towards its prey. POW! The heron's head hits the water and grabs the victim with its serrated bill. Great blue herons also eat frogs, salamanders, snakes, small birds, and mammals.

After eating, the heron cleans itself with the use of unique feathers called powder downs. These feathers continually disintegrate to a fine powder that the heron uses to clean or preen itself. This is done by combing the powder with the claw on the middle forward toe that has a comb-like inner edge.

When it comes time to mate, male herons develop back and neck plumes or aigrettes, and gather in heronries or colonies. Each male defends his territory in the tree where he plans to build his nest. Sometimes he'll reuse an existing nest once he has made the necessary repairs. Their nests, located high in trees, consist of twigs and branches about the diameter of a pencil. They are laid in what looks like a loose haphazard manor but in reality is constructed with care and ingenuity. Usually nests are about three feet in diameter. The inside area is about four inches deep by twelve inches in diameter and has softer vegetation to cushion the eggs.

The female heron lays three to five greenish-blue eggs and both parents share in the incubation. After about twenty-eight days, the eggs hatch and the parents begin to feed their young. At two weeks the young are able to stand upright and begin preening their feathers. By six weeks they begin preparing for their initial flight and begin to fly clumsily from tree to tree. At eight weeks they return to the nest only to feed. Finally, when they reach ten weeks they leave their nest for good and are independent.

The heron flies gracefully at speeds between nineteen and twenty-nine miles per hour with its neck folded back in an "S" shape with legs trailing behind. Its wings are broad and large having a wingspan of up to six feet.

Up to 69 % of newborn great blue herons die before the end of their first year from exposure, predators or accidents. The average life span is about seventeen years with the oldest known bird living to twenty-three years three months.

An interesting note about some great blue herons that live in south Florida is their color. It seems that there are white-phase great blue herons that are white like the great egret, but have light yellow colored legs and a blue mask on its face. At one time the great white heron was considered another species; however, dark and white young have been found in the same nest.

The only real enemy the adult great blue heron has is man. Habitat destruction by draining or flooding marshes and areas the bird uses for feeding is its greatest threat.

About the Author

John Harms II grew up in Palm Beach County, Florida when there were still wild areas left in the county. Many of his stories originate from his experiences as an active young boy. During that time he could be alone in a forest and enjoy the animals. Manatee and sea grasses were plentiful in the waterways by his home and deserted coconut plantations gave him a tropical background for his stories.

During his high school and college years, he became greatly concerned with the deterioration of the planet's ecosystem and began to study about it.

Graduating from University College at the University of Florida, he went on to design and patent filtration equipment at his father's company to purify water and other liquids.

Today, he devotes his time writing books for children, and doing presentations at schools. His themes help children take an interest in their environment. He does extensive research on all his animal characters so they are as factual as possible. He is totally involved in the designing and manufacturing of his books.

His life is shared with his wife, three children, three birds, two dogs, one cat, countless fish, and lots of turtles.

About the Illustrator

Wildlife artist & illustrator Robin Lee Makowski grew up in the suburbs outside Chicago which exposed her to a variety of wildlife. The bottlenose dolphins at Brookfield Zoo near Chicago fascinated her and sparked a life-long interest in marine mammals. Many of her illustrations have appeared in books, magazines and journals such as the Cousteau Society's *Dolphin Log, National Geographic Magazine, The New York Times,* and educational materials published by the Wild Dolphin Project and the American Cetacean Society.

Robin lived in Los Angeles, California for sixteen years where she met her husband Mark and they raised their boys, Vincent and Matthew. Her family frequently traveled to Baja California, Mexico to camp and observe the wildlife, including the Pacific gray whales. Moving to Hobe Sound, Florida in 1992 has given Robin another perspective on the local wildlife and problems related to pollution and habitat loss.

Robin considers her talents a gift to be shared and takes responsibility in educating the next generation in the care of their fellow creatures and the Earth we all must share.

Also read about Buster's first adventure in Book One:

The Saving of Arma Armadillo

by John Harms II

ISBN 0-9653871-1-9

Available through bookstores and Frederick Press

Look for these upcoming titles by John Harms II from Frederick Press:

Buster's third adventure:

The Saving of Sly Manatee

Manatee Freedom

and

The Mystery of No Name Island

Frederick Press
P. O. Box 32593
Palm Beach Gardens
Florida 33420
(561) 625-4964